For Annemarie,
Heleen

For Ellen and Sandra,
Peter

First American Paperback Edition 2006
First American Edition 2005
by Kane/Miller Book Publishers, Inc.
La Jolla, California

Original title: *Wil je me dragen?*
Copyright © text Heleen van Rossum
Copyright © illustrations Peter van Harmelen
First published by
© Zirkoon uitgevers, Amsterdam, The Netherlands 2004

All rights reserved. For information contact:
Kane/Miller Book Publishers
P.O. Box 8515
La Jolla, CA 92038
www.kanemiller.com

Library of Congress Control Number: 2004109115

Printed and bound in China by Regent Publishing Services, Ltd.

1 2 3 4 5 6 7 8 9 10

ISBN-10: 1-933605-22-7
ISBN-13: 978-1-933605-22-7

Will You Carry Me?

By Heleen van Rossum

Illustrated by Peter van Harmelen

Kane/Miller
BOOK PUBLISHERS

Thomas has been playing
in the park all morning.
He has been on the swing.
He has fed the ducks.
He has played hide and seek.

Now, it's time to go home.
And Thomas is very, very tired.

He stretches up his arms.
"I'm too tired to walk, Mommy. Will you carry me?"

Mommy looks at Thomas and smiles.

"Well, if you're too tired to walk, maybe we should try...

...JUMPING!"

She hitches up her pants
and bends her knees.
And then, she jumps.
She jumps past the pond.
She jumps through the grass.

And Thomas jumps right behind her.

But when they reach the park gate,
Thomas stops jumping.
He stretches up his arms.
"I'm too tired to jump anymore, Mommy.
Will you carry me?"

Mommy looks at Thomas.

"Well, if you're too tired to walk or jump,
maybe we should try...

...SWIMMING!"

She swims with her arms and kicks with her legs.

She swims past the school. She swims past the soccer field.
And Thomas swims right behind her.

But when they reach the crosswalk,
Thomas stops swimming.
He stretches up his arms.
"I'm too tired to swim anymore, Mommy.
Will you carry me?"

Mommy looks at Thomas and smiles.
"Well, if you're too tired to walk or jump or swim, maybe
we should try...

...FLYING!"

She sticks her nose straight up in the air and flaps her wings.

She flies past the shops.
She flies past the library.

And Thomas flies right behind her.

But when they reach the corner, Thomas stops flying.

He stretches up his arms.
"I'm too tired to fly anymore,
Mommy. Will you carry me?"

Mommy looks at Thomas and smiles.
"Well, if you're too tired to walk or jump or swim or fly,
maybe we should...

...RUN!"

Her eyes start to sparkle and her feet begin to bounce.
She chases Thomas. Thomas chases her.

And they run and laugh all the way down the street, until, finally, they are home.